SCOUT ALLEN

One of a Kind

Lesbian Erotica

WARNING

This book contains sexually explicit scenes and adult language. It may be considered offensive to some readers. This book is for sale to adults ONLY.

* * * * * * * * * * * * * * * * * *

Please store your files wisely where they cannot be accessed by underage readers.

Please feel free to send me an email. Just know that these emails are filtered by my publisher. Good news is always welcome.

Scout Allen - **scout_allen@awesomeauthors.org**

About the Publisher

4Fun Publishing, a member of **BLVNP Incorporated**, 340 S. Lemon #6200, Walnut CA 91789, info@blvnp.com / legal@blvnp.com
NOTE: Due to the highly emotional reaction of some people to works of erotic fiction, any email sent to the above address that contains foul language or religious references is automatically deleted by our anti-spam software and will not be seen. All other communications are welcome.

DISCLAIMER

Please don't be stupid and kill yourself. This book is a work of FICTION. Do not try any new sexual practice that you find in this book. It is fiction and not to be confused with reality. Neither the author nor the publisher or its associates assume any responsibility for any loss, injury, death or legal consequences resulting from acting on the contents in this book. Every character in this book is over 18 years of age. The author's opinions are not to be construed as the opinions of the publisher. The material in this book is for entertainment purposes ONLY. Enjoy.

One of a Kind
Lesbian Erotica

By: Scout Allen

© Scout Allen 2014
ISBN: 978-1-62761-772-7

SHE WALKED to the frame she was working on, torch and materials in hand. She placed them both down near the frame before welding.

A pink hardhat came up onto the welder and placed a toolbox down near her, waiting until she was finished, careful to keep his eyes away from the welder's spark.

"Hey, we finished work an hour ago. Let's go!"

Grunting as she finished, she flipped up her mask, and a female face looked at the male's, partially hidden underneath his pink hardhat. "Just finishing up the last touches," she told him with a smile. "You know how I am." She picked up her tools and took off the welder's mask, then twisted off the tanks of propane and acetylene.

"Okay, let's book it."

The pair walked off the construction site and into the same car, heading to the bar that they loved to go to. One for the food, the other for the waitress.

A smiling woman, just a year away from being thirty, greets the pair as they take a table in her section. It was a quiet Monday and they had air around them to talk.

"Hey Candice, Heath. How's it going?"

~=*0*=~

Leanne had been wondering when the two would show up; it was an hour later than when they usually showed up and she had been waiting to see her friend Candice, who always seemed to brighten her day.

"It's going good," replied Heath.

"A late finish today," explained Candice, "had to weld up a frame. I didn't want to leave it unfinished until tomorrow."

After her friend's explanation, she breathed a sigh of relief. She understood the dangers of their work, and her mind had concocted many horrible reasons why they hadn't shown up.

"Oh, well I'm glad it wasn't anything serious."

Leanne took their orders then went and punched them in, before checking on her other tables.

Heath watched the waitress go, pondering the worry he had caught in her voice.

When Leanne came back to them to talk about her morning - something about a horrible woman who had come in for lunchtime - Heath watched them without saying a word.

These two women, he observed, were seemingly opposites in their personality and lifestyles. But somehow, they had formed a bond that he wasn't sure they themselves were completely aware of. Leanne, with her uncertainties and turbulent emotions about anything that distressed her, was able to talk to Candice. In turn, Candice, with her steadfast sense of self and blunt way of dealing with her emotions, offered her advice in a very direct way that seemed to help her.

He was no stranger to watching the two women relate with each other. Yet over the last two months he'd seen something a little bit more intimate than normal. It started with a touch on the shoulder here and a playful swat there, and then Leanne would put her hand on Candice's leg for a moment longer than necessary. This part was most odd because Candice hadn't expressed an interest in women, at least she hadn't told him about it, but she never pulled away or asked Candice to remove it, and they would continue to talk normally as if it were natural.

Taking a drink of water, he noticed Leanne's hand disappear underneath the table to touch her friend's leg again and Candice gave her a warmer smile. Then they continued talking as if nothing had happened. He looked up at another waitress he knew well, one he was truly trying to move past the barrier of friendship with, and saw that she had seen as well. They exchanged looks of knowing.

That hand on her thigh, the one that felt immediately comforting without doing anything else was just one reason Candice loved her friend. Leanne had also helped her discover a more artistic side of herself, and her mind always seemed to clear of all worries, and her troubles seemed to flow away just because Leanne was there. These, among many others, were why she loved her friend.

What she was finding out only recently though, was that her feelings for Leanne, whom she'd helped with many a dick-headed boyfriend, was becoming something more than friendship.

Candice found Leanne so beautiful, with her long blond hair and a bust that rivaled her own, although Candice was more muscular. She always thought that Leanne's rounder frame looked more feminine and she would always admire how she looked.

"I'm sure she was just pissy because she was on her period," Candice said with a grin.

Leanne laughed out loud and her hand moved against Candice's leg, giving her shivers as it moved further up her inner thigh than before.

"You always know what to say," Leanne remarked, looking into her friend's eyes.

They held each other's gazes, before Leanne had to leave and attend to the other tables. She returned only to bring out the food for her friends and soon she was busy with cleaning up for the end of shift, leaving her little time to talk.

Candice politely waited for Leanne to finish. Heath had moved from his seat and was now talking with the other waitress, Alex. He was flirting quite obviously and she denied his every advance. It only made him try harder, but that was just the game. Heath was a conqueror, a man's man. It was good fun.

Alone, Candice watched Leanne as she went about the tables, taking away plates and bringing checks. Whenever the waitress would walk towards her, her eyes would watch Leanne's rolling hips, then when the waitress moved past her, her gaze would rise up to Leanne's bum. She consciously had to stop herself by taking another sip of her beer.

This had been going on for a while.

Candice never had many female friends; most girls she met weren't really interested in the same things as she was. In this Leanne was no exception, and when they'd first become friends she'd found it hard to listen to her talking about her day. It was teeth-gritting even, but now she listened more intently with true worry and concern for her friend. Leanne was easier to talk to and be with, for some reason.

She took another swig.

~=*0*=~

Leanne couldn't help but be attracted to Candice. She wasn't against being with women; in fact she had had girlfriends before and found them to be easier to understand than men. She knew that Candice had no interest in women, but she couldn't help but push the boundary of friendship between them, as she does whenever she touches her, or looks at her eyes, which she always loved to do.

When Leanne finished up, the two girls left together, leaving Heath to his fruitless conquest.

They ended back at Leanne's, as they had for a while now.

Leanne opened up a can of beer for her friend and grabbed a glass of wine for herself, and they began talking.

With alcohol flowing, inhibitions lowered and as usual, the conversation turned to their sex lives.

Candice had been out of a relationship with a guy for about six months and she just hadn't gone out to find another one. Part of it was because she was busy, surely, and if there were other reasons, she hasn't gotten around to sharing them yet. Maybe she wasn't sure either what it was.

Leanne, for her part, had just gotten out of another relationship with a guy. It lasted about three months, and he was just like the rest. Candice had helped her get rid of him with a right cross and a swift kick to the gonads.

"I just want to say again, thanks." It had only been a day, but it had also been five glasses of wine and seven beers later. She put her hand on her friend's thigh.

Candice looked at the hand for a second and Leanne, catching her glance, quickly backed off. The room went silent for a long moment as Candice reached for her eighth beer.

"No problem." She took a swig. "He was a dick."

Leanne nodded in agreement, reaching for her own drink.

Candice looked at her can of alcohol pensively, and her boundaries had apparently lowered to a point where she could ask this question. "Lee?"

"Hmm?" Leanne looked at her friend, intrigued by her tone.

"I was wondering…just out of curiosity…" she looked worried as she searched for words. "Why do you do that?"

Leanne, a little tipsy herself, asked: "Do what?"

"Go out with dicks like that?"

"Oh," Leanne had been hoping for something else. She was hoping Candice would say something like, 'put your hand on my leg all the time?'

"Well I can't seem to find the right guy." She grabbed her wine glass once more.

"Or girl?" Candice asked, hesitantly.

Leanne looked at Candice, "Or girl," she confirmed with a grin, taking another sip of her wine. Sliding closer to her she put a hand on her thigh once more. "Girls are easier to get along with."

Candice gulped down loudly. "Oh. Uh…" she squirmed. "I should go."

"Please stay," Leanne implored her friend, before she could get up.

Candice couldn't seem to say anything intelligible. Her mind was swirling with thoughts and images. But those two words struck a chord in her that she didn't want to admit existed.

"I probably shouldn't," she said and looked away, even as she remained where she was. Her nipples were getting hard at the thought of spending the night with Leanne, and her crotch was getting moist at the ideas in her mind.

"But it's late," Leanne protested. "I wouldn't feel right letting you go out like this." It was late, but not that late.

Candice looked outside for moment, thinking. If she wanted to know what she was really feeling for her friend, this was a good chance to find out.

"It is, isn't it?" She looked back at her friend and smiled. "Maybe just for once."

Leanne smiled and jumped up, "I'll get you some PJ's to wear." She rushed off.

Soon she returned wearing sleepwear of her own, a sleeveless tee paired with some boy shorts.

Candice gulped internally. Those long bare legs suggesting what they met at, that loose tee that left nothing to the imagination… she was getting wetter at the prospects. She felt very self-conscious about her thinner, not-as-curvy body compared to her friend's.

"Here," she handed her a similar outfit, "Sorry. I'm kind of bigger than you are," she said. "I'm not sure if these'll fit."

"It's ok," said Candice, "These'll do."

They didn't, not really, but she walked back out to the living room in a sleeveless tee that was hanging off her and she held onto the boy shorts to keep them up. She felt exposed.

~=*0*=~

Leanne was so wet it was showing through her shorts and her nipples were rock hard at the prospects that blushing Candice's loose garments suggested. "Come on, sit down."

Candice sat down and the shorts rode down a little. "Oh, sorry," she said, reaching for another beer. Cracking it open, she gulped down half of it quickly.

Leanne was grinning on the inside like a mad woman. She knew that this was it, now or never. "Um, Candice?"

"Yeah?"

She slid her hand onto Candice's bare thigh, and she felt the goose bumps rise all along the other woman's soft skin.

"I like you." Candice gulped.

Leaning in closer, her face inches from her friend's, Leanne didn't back off. "I really like you."

"I--" was all Candice got out as Leanne leaned in for a kiss.

Tongues danced with each other as their hands abandoned their drinks on the table and for the first time, Candice put her hand on Leanne's leg. The kissed ended and she looked into her friend's eyes. She looked scared.

"I've never done this before."

"It's ok, I'll show you how," Leanne reassured her, before going back to kissing her. Moving her hand across Candice's thigh, Leanne moved her fingers underneath Candice's shorts, inching closer to her burning sex.

~=*0*=~

Candice felt like a young girl again, exploring her own body for the first time.

Fingers brushed her bush and touched her slit. Gasping out loud, she broke the kiss and looked down at Leanne's fingers, easily underneath the large boxers. She threw caution to the wind and pushed down the offending garment. She blushed at her sudden nudity and boldness, which wasn't like her at all.

Leanne looked at her friend's beautiful pussy and ran her fingers up and down her lips. Candice sighed into her friend's embrace and tried to do the same for her but she was too caught up in the moment. Leanne didn't mind. Getting down on the floor she spread Candice's thighs and touched her clit with her fingers, slowly masturbating her.

"Oh, that's good."

Leanne moved her mouth in and breathed on her friend's cunt, sending shivers through her body. Leanne touched the lips with her tongue, running it up and down the length of Candice's slit. A loud moan came out from Candice's mouth. Leanne continued to rub her clit as she pushed her tongue slightly deeper and ran it up her slit again. A groan erupted from Candice again as she grasped her own breasts through the fabric of her shirt and twisted her nipples. "Yes… Yes."

Tucking her hair behind an ear, Leanne moved her mouth closer to her friend's bush and darted her tongue into her velvet entrance, again and again, faster and faster, electing gasps of ecstasy from her friend.

"Oh god yes, faster, faster…FASTER!" Candice cried out. She was practically mauling her own breasts now and, frustrated by the shirt in her way, she tore it off and sat nude before the friend who was now deep in between her legs. Leanne looked into her friend's eyes without stopping. Gasping for breath, Candice met her friend's steady gaze. "Oh god, I can't believe you're doing this! Ah, ah ah!"

Leanne tripled her efforts and soon Candice was screaming out loud as her friend brought her to a climax like never before.

She had clenched her legs together so tightly she nearly cut off Leanne's air. She loosened up and dropped them as she came down, dazed, sitting there with her eyes wide open and her mind well and completely blown. Leanne moved up her friend's body and was soon straddling her on the couch, "Do you want keep going?"

Not that she was completely sober, she was still a little bit drunk; but her mind had cleared enough for her to realize what she'd done, and what she wanted.

Saying nothing, Candice grabbed her friend's shirt and pulled it up and over her head and kissed her large firm breast right on her nipple. She wasn't sure what she was doing but she tried what worked best on her from experience with different lovers.

As she bit them, Leanne gave out a little squeal of pleasure. Candice then flicked it with her tongue, going up and down rapidly, as her hand reached down to Leanne's crotch to massage her burning lips.

"Yes right there, keep going. Yes!"

Moving to the other breast, Candice did the same thing and increased her speed. She was still half in a sexual haze herself, but fully determined to bring her friend off. Candice's tongue against Leanne's sensitive nipple sent shivers through her body.

Her friend, no her lover, was finally touching her, and she was getting off on the reality of it as much as the sensations shooting through her brain.

"Yes, yes, harder! Bite me!"

Candice followed her instructions and gave her nipple a sharp quick bite, making Leanne jump. She asked for it again and again Candice complied, making Leanne jerk against her friend's grip. Leanne felt Candice adjust her hands, moving them from her back to her ass, which she squeezed, boldly, making Leanne wonder if she liked asses.

The thought escaped her as Candice held onto her and pulled Leanne towards her hot sex.

Letting go of Leanne's nipple, Candice looked up at her friend's face. She had stopped masturbating for a second to give her a reassuring smile, before pulling off the only piece of clothing that separated their sexes. It was a little awkward to pull off but neither of them cared what happened to it in the moment. It soon flew across the room, leaving Leanne in her blond nakedness.

Candice looked at her nude friend for the first time. No wonder she attracted all the good looking guys! She was curvy, her breasts were firm and big enough to grab a handful of, and her ass, her best feature, Candice thought, was big and firm.

She looked like a fifties pinup girl, and she was on Candice's lap.

Touching her friend's slit, she rubbed her clit fast and Leanne helped her out verbally, "Faster, faster, yes!" She had bit her lower lip in sexual frustration, and grabbed Candice's nipple, giving it a pinch then gasping as two fingers entered her.

"Ohh yeah, fuck me," she moaned, "Finger fuck me!"

Candice, only being human, obeyed her and began thrusting both digits out like pistons, faster and faster. With each thrust, she felt a primal need awaking in her until she reached down and began masturbating herself too. She moaned, "ahhhh, ahhhh," and then she grabbed onto the couch behind her friend and rode her to climax.

Her arms shaking, she moaned out loud and then stopped suddenly. Leanne wasn't moving, and Candice was afraid she'd done something wrong.

Leanne suddenly looked at her with a smile on her face. "That was wonderful," she leaned in for a kiss. Girl cum ran down her legs to join her friend's, in a puddle on the couch.

She sat down beside her as they both basked in the afterglows of sex. Candice's head was awash with thoughts and feelings that she never knew she had for this woman. They just had sex together and her only regret was that they hadn't done it sooner. The combination of the feelings she had for this woman, coupled with Leanne's skills at eating her out, had made her cum like never before.

"Oh wow," she stroked her friend's thigh as they sat together, "That was amazing."

"It's not over yet," said a still unsatisfied Leanne.

Only being with a man who came once and that was it, Candice was pleasantly surprised. Her friend disappeared into her room and then came back with a box and some towels. She used one to wipe up the mess on her couch then put the second underneath her friend to protect the couch from their cum.

She then grabbed the box and sat beside her on the towel and opened it up. Candice's eyes widened. Leanne had a lot of sex toys.

A couple of vibrators and some dildos of varying sizes, a butt plug, some anal beads, a vibrating bullet, toy cleaner, lube and a strap-on dildo. Sure she had toys herself, but only a dildo she used frequently when she wasn't dating. It seemed Leanne was about to help her expand her mind.

"Here, lets us these." Leanne pulled two identical dildos and handed one to her friend and put the box on the table.

Masturbating, Leanne built a good rhythm until she was wet and ready, opening up her pussy. She slid in the dildo and began fucking herself with it. Candice was right with her, moving her dildo deep inside herself then back out till it was just the tip. She gave a moan of pleasure.

Fucking herself with the dildo faster, Candice leaned onto her friend's shoulder and gasped out loud as she fucked herself with the plastic phallus. Leanne watched her friend work herself into a frenzy as her own hand pistoned deep into her own, faster and faster. She touched her clit and sucked in a breath at how sensitive it was. Her little clit's hood was pulled back and she grasped the little button between her fingers and gave it a squeeze, making her jump and then moan. "Ohhhh!"

Candice was breathing heavily by this point and she began to pant as she was reaching another climax. "Ahh, ah. Oh fuck, I wanna be fucked," she looked at the box, "Fuck me!" she screamed as she came. Her body shuddered against her friend's, her chest heaving as she rode out the climax.

Leanne was right behind her as she screamed out loud, "Ahhh, yes, yes I'm cumming!" and she threw her head back, mouth open in a silent scream as her juices flowed out onto the couch. Afterwards she grabbed her friend and pulled her onto her lap so she'd have better access to her friend's breasts. She lowered her head and sucked on the erect nipples and touched her friend's clit with her fingers. Candice, needing her pussy filled, shoved her dildo back in and pumped her wet and ready snatch.

Candice was beside herself with pleasure as she rammed the dildo into her pussy, while Leanne's fingers rubbed her clit furiously back and forth, and Leanne sucked, bit and kissed her breast fiercely. Leanne then grabbed her other breast and groped her hard, paying attention to her sensitive erect nipples as she did.

Lust dominated Candice's mind and all she thought about was the need to get off.

~=*0*=~

Candice's screams and moans had the desired effect on Leanne. Her own crotch was getting wet and hot underneath Candice's back, creating a sexual cave beneath her friend's body that was ready to be fucked as well. Through an effort of will she kept at it, massaging Candice's clit and teasing her erect nipples, as Candice urged her on. "Oh yes, yes, bite them. Ahhhh!"

Candice came fiercely onto her friend's fingers, and Candice pushed the dildo deep in herself at the moment of climax, making her moan out more.

Leanne was so wet she was sure she'd soaked through the towel beneath them and stained the couch, but she didn't care. Saliva coating her lips, she pressed them against her friend's, and teased her breast at the same time. Candice's climax finished as they kissed.

Taking a few minutes to breathe, Candice sat up and then looked at her friend's crotch. Leanne was soaking wet and her erect nipples that were driving her mad.

"Ok, my turn." She went back to the box of toys and pulled out the strap-on dildo and looked at Leanne. "Turn over bitch, it's my turn."

Candice was grinning from ear-to-ear, and her pussy was leaking girl cum around the strap-on. Leanne liked this dominant side of her friend and she obeyed, turning onto her knees on the couch, her horny cunt up in the air for Candice to see.

Putting her hands on her friend's ass, Candice sucked two fingers and slipped them inside and finger fucked her. Leanne groaned out loud, pressing her head against the soft cushions in frustration. "Stop teasing me and fuck me."

Candice grinned and continued to finger fuck Leanne harder until her fingers were completely inside her and then she pulled out her soaked digits and sucked them clean. Lowering her friend's ass, she positioned her dildo at her soaking wet cunt and gently slid in. Out a bit then a few more inches in, out a bit and a few more inches, until she was up to the hilt in her friend's pussy.

Leanne was groaning out loud into the couch, gripping the cushions for dear life.

Candice got into the rhythm and began fucking her hard and fast. Bringing out the whole length and then thrusting it all back into her in one swift motion, the sounds of Leanne groaning in pleasure spurred Candice on. She thrust harder and faster than before and Leanne's groans turned to screams muffled by the cushions.

"You like that, you bitch?" she said with her hands pulling Leanne's ass onto her dick with each thrust, as Leanne pushed against the plastic cock with her hips on each thrust.

"Ah-ah-ah-ah," was her only response. The lust in her voice was answer enough.

Candice watched Leanne's body hump her own, that smooth silky skin, her curvy hips, and her blonde hair that was now flying all over the place, as she humped her friend's cock. It all helped to turn her on even more and seemed to make her rock hard nipples even harder.

"I'm-cumming," Leanne said in a gasp in between thrusts and Candice summoned up enough energy to go faster until Leanne finally came with a moan that seemed to bounce off the walls.

Burying her plastic dick into Leanne's body, Candice took a moment to rest, before pulling out and watching her friend's cum run out of her pussy and down her legs.

Leanne stayed still, not wanting to move as her climax finished.

After she was finished she sat down beside Candice and grabbed the fake dick with her right hand then leaned in and kissed Candice on the cheek. "You were a natural with this thing," shaking the dick for emphasis.

"Thanks," was all Candice could say.

Leanne curled up against her chest and stroked her while Candice stroked her thigh, as they both came down from their sexual high.

"So I guess this means we're dating?" said Candice with a smile.

Giving her friend a kiss, Leanne looked down at her breasts and ran her fingers gently over them. "I guess you're right," then she remembered to ask, "Does that bother you?"

Candice shook her head. "It used to, but now, after I know how good it is, and how good I feel finally doing this with you. No, it doesn't bother me."

She'd been completely honest with Leanne, and more importantly, with herself.

"But," Candice said and Leanne tensed right up, "It'll be different dating a girl instead of a guy."

Leanne could only laugh a little. "Not as different as you think."

They both sat there until the glow had worn off, then they showered, toweled down and went to bed nude, holding each other.

~=*0*=~

The next morning, Leanne woke up and looked at the strange mat of hair in front of her, which belonged to her friend-turned-lover, Candice. The sight of Candice's short, cute hair made her smile as she looked down to the face that was drooling,

"You are so cute sometimes," she said, tucking some hair behind her friend's ear for her.

Attempting to get up, she realized that her arms were caught underneath that black hair. "Oh come on sweetie, I've got to leave for work."

Sleeping Candice would not budge.

Leanne gave her a little shake and she groaned out loud, swatting at Leanne like she was an alarm clock.

"Wake up sleepy," Leanne coaxed. "You have to get to work too."

With a hand resting on her friend's chest, Candice finally woke up and looked into Leanne's eyes. "Oh," she looked around, and her face blushed as she remembered their night together. "Is it morning?"

Leanne grinned on the inside, it was too easy. She said in the calmest, most uninterested way, "No it's eleven, we slept in."

Candice's eyes went wide, "What!" she spun to face the clock and saw that it was only six. Leanne's a natural early riser. Candice's eyes narrowed and she said in an obviously annoyed tone masked with anger, "You're an ass."

Leanne could only laugh, "Yes, but it was worth it."

Candice swung her legs to the side of the bed and stretched, only barely aware she was nude, she slept nude normally anyway. Stopping, her mind went over what went on last night: she'd slept with her friend, and they were dating. It might have overwhelmed her if it hadn't been a work day.

"Well I've got to call Heath, what is there to eat around here?"

Leanne, pleased that her friend was taking this as well as she was, stood up and without putting anything on, walked to the kitchen. Candice, feeling self-conscious as always about her body, pulled on a purple robe she spied on the back of the bedroom door.

Leanne worked diligently in the kitchen pulling out a pan, some eggs, bacon and what looked like precut potato squares. Slipping on an apron, Candice openly admired her friend's body. She was still her friend even if she was her lover, she reminded herself "I didn't know you cooked."

"I still have my secrets" said Leanne, smiling at her new girlfriend.

Candice called Heath and asked him to pick her up in ten minutes, leaving scant little time to eat up her delicious meal. She then got dressed and gave Leanne an appreciative look up and down once more.

"I still can't believe I'm saying this," she said, kissing Leanne on the cheek, "bye, honey."

Grabbing a handful of Candice's ass, Leanne asserted she was still the bold, sexual woman in this relationship. "Hurry back."

Reluctantly, Candice left.

Work went by slowly for her, as Candice's mind apparently decided work was less important than fussing over this new relationship she found herself in. It's not that there was anything wrong with being with another woman. The more she thought about it the more it seemed natural, especially with Leanne. Yet those nagging thoughts of doubt she always had at the beginning of a dating experience crept up into her mind. Although few were founded, after all this relationship was built on a friendship.

At lunch, Leanne called her. "So I think we should actually go out on a date."

"Really?" asked Candice, and again the thought of being out with Leanne both frightened and excited her. "What did you have in mind?"

"Nothing fancy. That new Bob Baxter movie is out now…"

Candice liked that actor and didn't mind seeing this hunk of a man in theatres. "Okay."

"Alright, I'm working a morning shift today. Do you mind meeting me at my place?"

"No, of course not," Candice assured her.

"Ok, see you at around seven?"

"Sure." Looking at her watch, Candice figured she would be off at four today if nothing went wrong.

"Bye."

"Bye." She hung up to find the guys around the work table looking at her, all grinning like they knew what was going on.

Her eyes snapped to Heath. "You're an asshole."

He shrugged his shoulders, and putting his hands up in the air, said: "I couldn't help it!"

After work, and the bombardment of questions about her relationship with a girl, Candice was actually looking forward to getting away from men tonight.

At six-thirty she looked herself in the mirror. She was wearing her underwear and sighed out loud.

"What does she see in me?" she muttered to herself, before looking for something to make herself look sexy for her girlfriend, which still sounded weird to say out loud.

Finally, after much deliberation and mix-and-matching, she settled on a classic look, a plaid button-down shirt with a sleeveless white wife beater underneath and some tight jeans with sneakers. She looked at her hair and did it up as best she could then made sure she had her wallet and keys then went to pick up her date.

Leanne lived in an apartment building right downtown, which made her working at the restaurant convenient as it was also downtown, but that meant parking was hell and getting to her place meant a mini-maze of doom. Finally though Candice gave up looking for a parking spot, and stopped in the alley to call Leanne and tell her when she was outside so she could pick her up. It was five to seven.

"Ok," Leanne said and she was soon outside, in a dress.

Candice couldn't take her eyes off her. The dress was blue and had a fancy pattern on it but Leanne was filling it out in a way she'd never thought about before. Her chest was pressing at the cups showing just the perfect amount cleavage to get Candice's attention without being revealing. Her long shapely legs went up and disappeared underneath the dress at mid-thigh, her high heels perking her chest up even more. She might as well have been wearing nothing the way it affected her in her cowgirl look.

Hopping in the car, she had to look at the road before she realized she was staring, "We going?"

"Oh uh, yeah." They took off.

They got popcorn and some drinks then went inside just as the previews were starting. They took a back row because Candice liked being at the top of the theatre.

Seeing as it was a Tuesday and there were maybe just five other people there, they were practically alone. The movie started and both women watched the main character Bob Baxter very closely, each one fanaticizing the man doing different things to them, in different positions.

"He is so hot," commented Leanne, reaching into her friend's lap for the popcorn.

"I'd love for him to just take me and throw me down," said Candice. Suddenly aware of her date, she said, "Not that you're not-"

Leanne put her hand on her friend's thigh comfortingly. "I'm not gay, sweetie, I'm bi."

"Right, sorry," she said and continued watching, noticing though that Leanne's hand hadn't moved.

The movie quickly moved to a romance scene and Leanne slid her hand up Candice's leg to her hot thighs and closer to her sex.

"Leanne," said Candice. "What are you doing?"

"Shhh," was all Leanne could reply, and rubbed her thigh for emphasis.

That gave her thoughts not of the main character but of her lover sitting beside her.

"Sorry," she said nonchalantly and spread her legs to give Leanne better access. What was she doing? She was never this bold with guys! Leanne seemed to bring out the exhibitionist in her.

Putting her hand onto the bare thigh of her lover, Candice looked into her eyes for a second, as both shared a look that could have painted a dozen lust-filled pictures. Turning their attention back to the movie, each moved their hand up only in response to the other's movement. Soon their hands where so hot and nipples so hard they would have ripped each other's clothes off right there, if not for the few others in the theatre.

"I've got to go to the washroom," said Leanne in a whisper.

This was one thing but, "Right now?"

"Yeah, it'll be quiet. No one will know," she said quickly.

Gulping down, Candice nodded before her brain knew what she was doing.

They quickly made their way down to the women's washroom and took the handicap stall, and Leanne without ceremony pulled Candice in for a kiss, lust thick in the air between them.

Candice, quickly getting used to the idea of being with a woman, slipped her hand underneath Leanne's dress and into her burning sex. A small gasp escaped Leanne's mouth but she continued kissing Candice anyway. Kicking off her heels, she pulled off Candice's plaid shirt and tossed it beside the toilet and then unzipped her lover's jeans.

Candice backed off for a minute, allowing Leanne to open her jeans to reveal her plain white cotton panties and then they went back to kissing. Leanne cupped her friend's sex and slipped in two fingers to furiously masturbate her.

The taboo nature of where they were, and the still new feelings of a being with a woman, drove Candice crazy as she kissed her friends lips to stop from crying out. Leanne played her friend's clit like a violin and she was soon cumming into her underwear with a moan she let out. Candice, still in her orgasmic glow, pulled down Leanne's dress, noticing she hadn't been wearing a bra tonight, and kissed one breast, flicking her nipples with her tongue the giving them a bite like she had before.

It had the desired effect as Leanne groaned out loud in response and then covered her mouth to stop her from getting too loud herself.

Alternating between nipples, Candice soon slipped down Leanne's underwear, discovering it was a thong. "You dirty girl. You wanted this," said Candice with a feral grin.

"You have no idea how much cowgirls turn me on," Leanne breathed and pulled her in for another kiss as she began humping her friend's fingers. The two women pressed into a wall with Candice's back and she kept her fingers going. In and out, in and out, Leanne's climax building on the horizon, while the soft beams of light that was her pleasure touched her deeply. Leanne moaned out loud, no longer able to keep kissing her lover in silence. "Yes, yes, faster, deeper!"

Candice's fingers soaked and her mind was a haze of lust in the need to fuck Leanne as if her fingers were a dick.

"Oh god," Leanne groaned out loud and leaned her head down next to Candice's, "put one in my ass."

"Okay." Not wanting to stop, Candice licked another finger and then slid it up into Leanne's rear entrance without any premise or warning.

Leanne groaned out loud and pulled her dress up and over her head, making her practically naked as they continued to fuck in the bathroom stall. With Candice sticking out her tongue and licking at Leanne's clit, she came loudly.

"Ahhh!" she collapsed to the floor, that filthy filthy floor. She then looked up at Candice with lust.

Pulling down Candice's panties, Leanne brought her lover down to the floor with her and then ripped off her own and pulled her pussy to Candice's. They mashed our crotches – both burning with desire-together, rubbing each other like mad women. Candice's gasp came out loud as she pulled up her top and grabbed her breast, sighing into the experience.

"Yeah fuck me, you bitch," she said, gritting her teeth into the words.

They ground their pussies together and Candice's body reacted in kind, making her smile and groan in response to the feeling of 'fucking' her girlfriend.

'My girlfriend,' Candice thought lustily. 'No one else's, this blonde Swedish bombshell with a body like I wanted but couldn't have is fucking my pussy with hers.'

"Oh god yes," she moaned out loud.

Candice's climax was building hard and long as she was on her second, her body tingled and her pussy tightened as she came up to kiss Leanne, and Leanne came up to kiss her back. Their hands viciously rubbed each-others clit as they moaned out loud, cumming together.

Candice felt her sex burn for more attention as Leanne bent down, naked in this bathroom stall and lapping at her cum. "Tasty," she looked at Candice. "You're nearly naked."

Throwing off her shirt, Candice declared, "Now I am."

With both women naked in a public bathroom stall, anyone curious enough could just look under and see them both naked and fucking as if possessed.

"Lick me, yeah lick me, you nasty bitch on this filthy floor!"

They were lucky no one was coming to investigate. Yet it didn't really register very much in their minds.

$$\sim=*0*=\sim$$

Leanne was an expert and worked Candice like some kind of master pussy licker, her tongue inside and running around Candice's pussy while teasing her clit with her fingers. Leanne held her lover's naked ass on the bathroom floor, pulling her closer. Candice helped her by humping her face enthusiastically, wanting more as the pressure of pleasure was building.

"Yes, deeper, go deeper!"

Candice could have sworn Leanne's tongue grew three inches as she pushed her face against Candice's body, practically suffocating herself as Candice came loudly on her face.

"Oh yes, you horny bitch!"

Patting Leanne's head as she came up, they then shared Candice's juices in a passionate kiss. Grabbing Leanne's ass, Candice pulled her onto her lap as they finished their kiss, naked in a movie theatre bathroom.

Breaking the kiss, Leanne smiled. "Oh, you were great."

"So where you" Looking around, Candice said, "Now let's go finish that movie."

"Hold on," said Leanne, grabbing her purse on the floor, bending over and showing off her perfect ass and pussy lips. She pulled out a vibrating bullet and its twin. "Here" she gave Candice one and then set hers low and slipped it in her pussy. "Oh yes, that's perfect."

Wear a vibrating bullet while watch a movie? Candice couldn't believe it. 'I'll cum into my panties during the movie!' she thought.

"Okay," she said and turned it on low and slipped it into her pussy as well.

The two women got dressed; in Leanne's case she simply slipped on her dress and shoes, and they walked back to the movie. No staff stopped them on the way, as Candice half-expected they would.

They sat down and watched the movie, the buzz in their pussies working them over as they watched the sculpted body of Bob Baxter move across the screen. Candice imagined he was fucking her as Leanne sat beside her, with and her body squirmed in her seat. Leanne, as if sensing her thoughts, grasped Candice's thigh and rubbed up and down her inner thigh, making her squirm all the more.

"Stop it."

But Leanne whispered in her ear, "Close your eyes and pretend it's him" she said, "I will if you'll do the same for me."

It took Candice but a nanosecond to think about it. "Okay."

Candice's hand touched Leanne's inner thigh and she closed her eyes, thinking about Bob Baxter using a vibrating dildo on her while touching her there. Soon, her breathing turned ragged and so did Leanne's.

Candice's nipples screamed for someone to touch them. A shuddering climax, though not as powerful as the one she had earlier, came over her.

This happened throughout the movie.

By the time they left, their panties were soaked, and cum ran down their legs.

They got in the car and quickly pulled out their bullets and then kissed. Leanne took the one that had just come from Candice's body and sucked on it like it was a fine delicacy. Taking hers, Candice greedily sucked off all the juices on it and then handed it back to her.

"You're just a horny little minx, aren't you?" accused Leanne with a grin.

Grinning like a mad woman, she put them away in her purse. "I like to think so."

This was going to be a great relationship.

THE END

Here is a sample from another story you may enjoy:

Scout Allen

EVERYTHING
I Wanted to Do

STEAMY HETEROTIC SEX

IT HAD been a month since the new laws regarding public nudity and public displays of sexuality had passed, and I'm still coming to terms with how fast the world was coming to terms with its new found freedom. Especially at my new job.

Guys would walk around without shirts and women would open up their blouses to reveal their bra clad chests, some would even go so far as bottomless or in their underwear. I guess I was lucky seeing as they were all in very good shape, a company mandate, we all were required to maintain a three day a week workout schedule. The boss said that a healthy efficient body was a healthy efficient mind.

The only problem was that all these semi-nude bodies were making me horny. That normally wouldn't be a problem, except that I'm not a normal woman.

I'm not lacking in the looks department, I'm a full bodied curvy black woman with a chest that would make most women jealous. But below the waist I'm not like other women, and it's not like it's a new thing, I've been this way forever.

I've got a woman's figure, and a man's plumbing. Like most people of my ethnic persuasion my ancestors left me rather well-endowed. At ten inches long and two across I've made more than a few guys embarrassed when they come to bed, full knowing what I am, and see that I'm bigger than they are.

I'm by no means a virgin, or particularly shy about my sexuality, but I didn't get to where I am by announcing to the world that I can compete in any pissing match the guys can.

Being the Regional Manager for the Brick stores in Western Canada, I'm definitely not low on the office totem pole, and that kind of title carries with it some dignity and respect I just can't afford to lose by showing how big my balls are.

Tiffany walked into my office, wearing a matching teal thong and bra. A redhead with full curves and legs that went on forever, it was hard having her as a secretary.

She smiled at me wearing only a knee length black skirt and panties myself. "The proposal from marketing is here" as she put down a file on my desk, "As well as Edmonton's, Vancouver's, Victoria's and our own numbers for this quarter" placing the next four down on my desk.

Giving her a smile, "Thank you Tiffany that'll be all"

Standing there for a moment she commented, for what seemed to be the millionth time. "Are you sure you're comfortable in that skirt? It's awfully hot in here"

It was true.

The CEO had turns off the AC for the summer as an excuse to save money. Yet everyone knew it was get the staff in the current state they were in. Everyone knew his orientation as it was and it was well known that he swung both ways. Of course it was one of those things everyone knew and no one talked about. A very unusual way for a boss to run his company, I know, but it seemed to work for him and the company.

Smiling up at Tiffany, who had told me the very first day she'd started for me she was into women, "I'm fine Tiffany, thank you" and turned back to my computer.

She looked down to my full breasts, as she had in the past few days, and smiled, practically licking her lips. "Alright then" and she left closing the door behind her.

The problem was that her advances weren't unwanted. In fact if we were anything but secretary and boss I would gladly respond to her advances. Yet despite all the secretaries I'd had over the years, even the few male ones, I'd never made a move towards them, in the name of professional courtesy.

Underneath my skirt the bulge was getting harder to ignore, with each passing day Tiffany was getting harder and harder to resist. Her firm pert breasts, while not as large as my own, where firm and inviting, that ass of hers she insisted on showing off made my mouth water each time she turned to leave. Stiff as a board practically every day it was harder and harder to get some work done without touching myself.

Today had been too much though, and the moment she'd left my hands unzipped my skirt and pulled down my boxers and sighed as my erect member touched air. Grasping my dick I gave it a few quick strokes as my mind brought back the images of Tiffanies ass and her barely covered breasts.

I needed this. It had been building for weeks. After each day I'd masturbated at least three times at home just to feel normal again. Those firm chests, breasts, penis's, pussies, at least one couple having sex at lunch each day, I'd had to start taking lunch in my office…

If you enjoyed this sample then look for <u>Everything I Wanted to Do</u>.

Also by this Author

About the Author

I've been writing for about thirteen years now but have never published anything, until recently.

I'm open for some creative criticisms to help move my stories from young hopeful to mature writer.

I LOVE playing video games, yes criticize me if you want but I love them, and my favorite original game is Assassin's Creed for putting the assassin in a position of honor and heroics. Some of my greatest influences come from video games, pictures, movies, books, random things like how something looks at a particular part of the day, manga, and anime.

Anime is the Japanese animated cartoons; Manga is the paper version (I hate it when people get it mixed up) and I like the ridiculousness of them and the imagination put into them because it's nothing like any cartoons you find in Canada. There's a freedom of expression in it I find so freeing, I dare you to tell me of another culture as expressive.

I obviously love writing, and I also like reading but find it very hard to find books that are engaging. Unless a book captures my attention right off the bat, I tend not to read it and it gets put on the backburner of my "to read" list.

I love listening to music when I write stories and often play scenes of my stories in my mind, mainly the action ones. It really helps me visualize them and get a good feel for them.

I like most music, even rap and country ones that I think people judge too harshly. And I draw inspiration from them as well.

As always read, live, laugh, and enjoy life to the fullest whenever you can. Peace!

Check my page on Amazon and my blog for Updates and interesting info.

Author Central - http://www.amazon.com/Scout-Allen/e/B00A48L3EU
Author Blog - http://scout-allen.awesomeauthors.org/

If you enjoyed any of my books then please share the love and click like on my books in Amazon.

If you write me a review and send me an email I will send you a free book, or many.
(Just know that these emails are filtered by my publisher.)

Good news is always welcome.

One Last Thing, For Kindle Readers...

When you turn the page, Kindle will give you the opportunity to rate this book and share your thoughts on Facebook and Twitter. If you enjoyed my writings, would you please take a few seconds to let your friends know about it? Because... when they enjoy they will be grateful to you and so will I.

Thank You!

Scout Allen
scout_allen@awesomeauthors.org